Frances Fyfield is a criminal lawyer, although she now only practises part-time. She lives in London, and in Deal, by the sea which, aside from her love of London, is her passion. Her previous novels have garnered acclaim and awards, and have been widely translated.

THE NATURE
OF THE BEAST

FRANCES FYFIELD

timewarner
paperbacks

A *Time Warner* Paperback

First published in Great Britain in 2001
by Little, Brown

This edition published by Time Warner Paperbacks in 2002

A CIP catalogue record for this book
is available from the British Library.

ISBN 0 7515 3231 2

Typeset in Plantin by M Rules
Printed and bound in Great Britain by
Clays Ltd, St Ives plc

Time Warner Paperbacks
An imprint of
Time Warner Books UK
Brettenham House
Lancaster Place
London WC2E 7EN

www.TimeWarnerBooks.co.uk